MEOWS AND MURDER

LATTE'S MEWSINGS COZY MYSTERIES, BOOK 1

PATTI BENNING

SUMMER PRESCOTT BOOKS PUBLISHING

Copyright 2020 Summer Prescott Books

All Rights Reserved. No part of this publication nor any of the information herein may be quoted from, nor reproduced, in any form, including but not limited to: printing, scanning, photocopying, or any other printed, digital, or audio formats, without prior express written consent of the copyright holder.

**This book is a work of fiction. Any similarities to persons, living or dead, places of business, or situations past or present, is completely unintentional.

CHAPTER ONE

Lorelei French always thought she had a normal life. She had a job that she loved, a small house she would be paying the mortgage on for another thirty years, a string of somewhat disappointing boyfriends, a strained but loving relationship with her mother, a handful of close friends with a wider circle of vague acquaintances that came and went, and a pet cat.

Of these, the cat, a petite, green-eyed feline with a coat the color of coffee, was probably the least normal feature of her life. It wasn't that the cat was a Havana Brown, though the breed was rare, that made her so unusual. Rather, it was the fact that she had an uncanny sense for when someone was about to die.

Or, that was what the nursing home had told Lorelei when she went to pick her up.

Latte, which Lorelei had named the kitten on impulse when she first saw her, had come from a breeder three hours away, and had been a gift for her grandmother on her eighty-fifth birthday. In retrospect, a slightly older and less energetic feline might have been a better companion for the elderly, wheelchair-bound woman, but Lorelei had been seized by impulse when she saw the ad for the kittens. Maybe it was bad judgment, or maybe it was fate. Either way, Latte seemed to bond immediately with both the older and younger woman and there had never been any question of not keeping her, even after she shredded the curtains at the nursing home. Twice.

Unfortunately, while Lorelei's grandmother, an impressive woman named Ethel Melrose, lived to see her ninetieth birthday, she hadn't lived to see her ninety-first. By then, the nursing home had ceased their complaints about the now six-year-old cat and had gently asked Lorelei whether she might let them keep her. Ethel Melrose's will had been very clear on the matter, however. Latte was to belong to Lorelei and Lorelei alone. Not prepared to go against the beloved older woman's last wishes, Lorelei showed up at the nursing home, armed with a cat carrier and a brand new litter box in the back of her car, three days after her grandmother's funeral to take the cat home.

That was when she first heard the rumors about Latte. Looking back, she decided she must have simply been oblivious prior to that visit, because news of the cat's sixth sense didn't seem to be any sort of secret at all. Even her mother, she would learn later, had heard of it.

"Are you sure you want to take her?" the somewhat weedy and bumbling head of staff, Mr. Bath, asked as he escorted her to her grandmother's room. "She's very special, you know. And a cat is a lot of responsibility."

Lorelei, now a good few months past the age of thirty, rather felt that she could handle the responsibility of a cat, and said as much. "And I know she's special," she added with a smile, trying to make up for the irritation of her first response. "I've never met a cat like her."

He unlocked the door to her grandmother's room, which had been left mostly untouched for the time being, and Latte darted out, immediately winding around Lorelei's ankles. Lorelei crouched to pet her, then glanced up at Mr. Bath. He was watching them with a morose expression.

"I can get you another cat for the nursing home," she volunteered, beginning to feel a bit bad. She wasn't sure why; it wasn't as though none of the other residents had cats, and really, he shouldn't be guilting her over taking her grandmother's pet home.

He shook his head. "It wouldn't be the same. Latte's... special."

"You said that already." She frowned, straightening up with said cat in her arms. "I'll take good care of her, you know. I've known her all her life. It's not as though she'll be living with a stranger."

"It's not that." He hesitated, looking at the cat in her arms. "What did your grandmother tell you about her?"

Truly puzzled now, Lorelei took some time to think about it. "Well, she likes cat food with salmon in it, but despises tuna. She likes cat nip, but goes a bit crazy if she has too much." Thus, the curtains. They had only repeated that mistake once. "And she's very demanding about her litter box being kept clean."

He looked pained. "So… you don't know?"

"I don't know what?"

He glanced at the cat, then back to her again. "Just keep an open mind while I explain, Ms. French." Lorelei considered her mind to be very open — it was a detriment, if she listened to her mother — and gave him a sharp nod to continue. "Latte knows when one of the residents is about to pass. She sticks to them like glue for the whole day, and she hasn't been wrong yet. It's uncanny, really. We were all a bit… disturbed by it, at first, but the residents take comfort from her. They like to know they won't be alone, at the end, and a few times it's given us a chance to get their relatives in for a final goodbye. I know what it sounds like, but ask anyone here and they'll tell you the same. I'm not a superstitious man by nature, but even I can see that she's something special."

Mr. Bath, in his buttoned-up shirt, pressed pants, and carefully shined shoes indeed did not give off the impression of a tendency toward superstition. Lorelei considered this, looking down at the cat in her arms, who had begun to purr.

"Well," she said slowly. "Even if that's the case, I'm

still going to take her. I'm sorry, I really am. I can see why you'd want her to stay. But it's in my grandmother's will, you see, and she's done so much for me over the years, and she asked for so little in return. I really don't think I can go against what she wanted for Latte."

He gave a resigned nod and sighed. "At least you know, now. Take care of her, Ms. French. She's given a lot of people comfort over the years."

"I will," she promised.

And that was how Lorelei ended up with a somewhat peculiar cat in her otherwise normal life. Eventually she reached an agreement with the nursing home, so Latte could stay with them whenever she went out of town, which she did relatively often to visit her mother, who lived a couple of hours away. It saved Lorelei boarding fees, and it gave the residents the chance to dote on Latte, who was never one to turn away extra attention.

Six months later, Lorelei's life was still rather normal. Her coffee shop, which she had opened with some financial assistance from her grandmother years before, was doing well, and Latte had yet to shred any curtains, though Lorelei had been careful to be stingy with the catnip.

In fact, she thought as she went over the budget during a lull on a sunny summer day, her red hair drawn up into a ponytail, *we're doing better than well.* French Roast was the most modern shop in all of Wildborne, Wisconsin, and it seemed to call to clientele from all walks of life. Lorelei was certain that every resident of the town had been inside at least once, and many were dedicated regulars. She had no illusions that a large part of her shop's popularity was simply due to the fact the only other place to get coffee in town was at the local diner. Deborah's Diner had the unique ability to make even the freshest grounds taste like instant coffee by the time they were done with them, so when it came to competition, French Roast didn't really have any. Even Deborah herself — not the original owner of the diner, she made sure to tell everyone that her name was just a happy coincidence — was a regular at French Roast.

The tiny bell over the door chimed, and Lorelei looked up from the spreadsheet on her laptop to see a welcome and familiar face come in. On her cat bed in the sunny windowsill, Latte raised her head and gave a pleased meow.

"Oh, there's my little muffin. Look at you; you've got the best spot in the house, don't you?"

Lorelei looked on in amusement as her friend cooed over Latte, who was happily soaking up the attention. Eventually, she cleared her throat. "It's good to know that you're really only friends with me for my cat, Alyssa."

Alyssa Figgins had been her friend since French Roast first opened. In fact, she had been Lorelei's first employee. Unfortunately, the woman didn't have a lick of instinct when it came to making anything edible or drinkable taste good, and couldn't remember a recipe to save her life, so the business aspect of their relationship ended pretty quickly. Thankfully, the friendship part was still going strong.

"Just the cat and the coffee," Alyssa corrected her with a smile. "Speaking of, please tell me you have it."

She approached the counter with a look of desperation in her eyes, ignoring Latte's meow of annoyance that the petting was over. Lorelei recognized the expression on her friend's face, and bit back the playful denial she had been planning.

"I have it," she admitted instead. "After I found a hundred and fifty notes in my suggestion box demanding I bring back the Salted Caramel Macchiato permanently, I knew I couldn't disappoint all of my faithful customers." Already reaching for the mini fridge where she kept the dairy, she shot her friend a look that was supposed to be unimpressed, but probably came across as amused. "Oddly enough, all one-hundred and fifty notes had the same handwriting."

"How strange," Alyssa said blandly, blinking twice before giving her a cheery smile. "Did you have your reading glasses on? I know how you hate to wear them. Perhaps you made a mistake."

Lorelei aimed a glare at the other woman, not even looking at her hands as she heated a small pot of milk and dulce de leche caramel on the electric burner behind the counter. Alyssa well knew how much she despised any mention of her reading glasses.

"You know, for someone whose friend is making a

new, permanent addition to the menu just for her, you're walking on pretty thin ice."

"Oh, fine," Alyssa said, watching eagerly as Lorelei hit the button to turn the espresso machine on and poured the milk and caramel mixture into a mug while it ground the beans. "You have perfect eyesight, I don't know a thing about the glasses-that-shall-not-be-mentioned, and I admit it. I wrote all of the notes. You're the best friend in the whole world, Lorelei."

"I know I am," Lorelei said smugly. She poured the espresso into the mug then paused to whip up a small batch of whipped cream, then topped the resulting drink in a drizzle of caramel syrup and a sprinkle of coarse salt. "There you go. And if you want another, it will be decaf."

Alyssa gave her a mildly hurt look, but took the mug gratefully, nonetheless. She knew as well as Lorelei just how hyper too much caffeine made her, and no longer even complained about the fact that she was the one customer who had a hard cut-off limit.

As Alyssa sipped her drink in a state of bliss, Lorelei cleaned up her station then risked a glance at the clock. Almost closing time. She winced. There was a huge pile of laundry waiting to be folded at home, and she much preferred making coffee to that, but she knew that every man, or woman, in this case, had to face their demise eventually. She had only wished she might have a better end than being smothered by shirts and socks, done to death by her own procrastination.

"Here," she said, unceremoniously tossing a rag at her friend. "You get the tables, I'll get the rest?"

Alyssa gave a cheery enough nod, as Lorelei knew she would. The other woman knew well where all of her free coffee came from, and she wasn't about to irritate the source too much. "Just as soon as I finish up here." She took another sip of the coffee and closed her eyes with a sigh.

Lorelei gave a fond shake of her head, which her friend didn't see, and left her to enjoy her coffee while she got started on the kitchen. She knew by the time she came out, the tables would be spotless, and the caffeine in the drink would have likely spurred Alyssa to help out even more. As long as it was guided, her friend's susceptibility to caffeine could be very useful indeed.

CHAPTER TWO

Once the coffee shop was clean and ready for opening the next morning, Lorelei and Alyssa went their separate ways, saying goodbye just outside the back door. Alyssa lived in an apartment over an antique shop just down the block, so her walk home would be over in no time at all, and it would help her burn off some of that extra energy. When she first moved there, Lorelei had been worried about her new friend walking home alone at night, but she quickly realized that it was perfectly safe. Nothing ever happened in Wildborne.

Lorelei approached her car; an old, two-door sky blue convertible. The soft top was far from ideal, given Wisconsin winters, but it had been a college gift from her father, and she was too attached to it to sell it.

Thankfully, Latte's wire cat carrier fit in the cramped back seat perfectly. She set the carrier down now, making sure it was wedged between the front and back seats so it wouldn't shift too much when she inevitable took the turn into her driveway too quickly, then buckled herself in.

The street she lived on was called Honey Bee Street, which was what had drawn her to the house in the first place, though she would never admit to anyone. Her grandfather had kept bees before he passed away, and she had always had a fondness for them. The house itself was pale yellow, with a pale pink house on one side and a blue one on the other. It was a colorful street, with colorful residents. Lorelei realized she was going to have to intervene between two of the more colorful ones when she swung into the driveway that always seemed to sneak up on her, thanks to her neighbor's overgrown pine tree, and saw two women talking on the porch of the pink house.

Both women paused to wave at her as she parked in front of the detached garage — she used the term garage loosely, because it wasn't quite big enough to fit even her small car — then returned to their very animated argument.

She got out of the car and headed over to them reluctantly, but with a feeling that it was her duty. Her immediate neighbor, Mrs. Whittaker, was an exceedingly elderly woman who somehow managed to not only have avoided a nursing home, but also kept a better garden than anyone else on the street did. The woman who lived one door down from Mrs. Whittaker was Marigold Marsters. She was one of the few people Lorelei simply couldn't bring herself to like, no matter how hard she tried. Everyone who knew her seemed to share that sentiment, so she didn't feel too badly about it.

"Lorelei," Mrs. Whittaker said when she spotted her approaching. "How lovely of you to join us. What do you think of my new gardenias?"

Lorelei made a show of examining the pretty white flowers planted on either side of the small porch. Marigold was giving her a hard look, but she ignored it; she much preferred Mrs. Whittaker, and the older woman seemed glad for her interference.

"They're beautiful and they smell lovely," she said, straightening up. Mrs. Whittaker beamed. Marigold glared.

"They smell awful," she snapped. "I've never liked the scent of gardenias, and now the smell blows right into my kitchen window every morning!"

"The poor things were withering outside of Con's," Mrs. Whittaker replied calmly. Con's was short for Constantine's, which was what everyone called their local grocery store. The store was actually named Fresh Goods Grocery, which had lent itself to a lot of confusion when Lorelei first moved there. "They're just starting to get some life to them now. If I move them, they may not be able to bounce back a second time."

"I don't care. The smell is making me sick." Marigold narrowed her eyes. "Take care of it."

Without saying a word to Lorelei, she turned and stalked back toward her house. Lorelei and Mrs. Whittaker exchanged a look and a strained smile, then Lorelei gestured back toward her car.

"I've got to go get Latte in and start on dinner. It was nice talking to you, though." She paused, then grinned. "The gardenias really are lovely. I'll leave my windows open this evening. With any luck, the wind will blow the other direction, and my house will be the one that smells like flowers."

Mrs. Whittaker gave a quiet laugh. "You're a sweetheart. Thanks for the rescue. Do you want blueberry or apple this Sunday?"

Lorelei thought about it. "Apple. With cinnamon?"

"Have I ever disappointed?"

"Nope." She grinned. "I'll see you then."

Every Sunday, she and Mrs. Whittaker had an early breakfast together. Lorelei supplied the tea, courtesy of French Roast, and the older woman made fresh scones or muffins. Since the coffee shop didn't open until later on Sundays, it was the perfect way to start the day.

Lorelei hurried Latte inside, where she set the carrier on the floor and let the meowing cat out. Latte gave her a vaguely insulted look, as if she couldn't believe her owner had made her wait in the car for all of five minutes, then ran over to the small end table that was dedicated to her food and water dishes.

"I get the message." She opened a cupboard and withdrew two cans of cat food. Reading the labels, she asked, "Salmon and chicken, or rabbit?" She held the cans out for inspection. Latte sniffed both carefully, then rubbed her head against the salmon and chicken one. Taking this as a sign of approval, Lorelei opened the can and emptied it into the cat's empty food bowl.

With her smaller companion's meal sorted, Lorelei pulled open the fridge to see what she could make for herself. The sound of the mail truck caught her attention before she could make her choice, and she let the fridge fall shut as she slipped her feet into the sandals she kept by the front door and went outside.

As soon as she opened the front door, Latte dashed out between her feet. Lorelei, who could have sworn the cat was still eating her dinner, made a too-slow grab for her. Grumbling to herself, she watched as the cat darted toward Mrs. Whittaker's house. She spotted Latte rubbing herself across the older woman's ankles, and decided to go ahead and get the mail first. Mrs. Whittaker liked the cat, and never complained about the occasional visits when the feline snuck outside.

After retrieving the sheath of junk mail and bills from the mailbox, she walked up the path to her neighbor's house, where the elderly woman was still petting

Latte. Not expecting trouble, she said, "Sorry, she slipped out when I opened the door," as she bent to pick up the cat.

Unexpectedly, Latte hissed at her, arching her back and fluffing out her tail as if she was taking part in a Halloween skit. Lorelei jumped, and straightened up immediately, feeling strangely hurt. Latte had never hissed at her before.

"Oh, why don't you let her stay?" Mrs. Whittaker said. "She can spend the evening here, and I can bring her over in the morning. She visits often enough already; she might as well start having overnights. I've still got a spare cat box somewhere from when Mr. Buttons was alive, and I'm planning on shrimp salad for dinner. I know how much she likes shrimp, and I won't mind the company, to be honest."

Lorelei hesitated, not because she didn't think the older woman would take good care of Latte, but because she suddenly remembered what Mr. Bath had said half a year ago. She hadn't yet seen any indication that Latte was anything but a very smart cat, but a bad feeling had settled over her at the sight of Latte's utter refusal to leave Mrs. Whittaker's side.

"Are you sure?" she asked reluctantly.

"Positive. Unless you'll miss her too much, of course. But I've been feeling lonely lately; having some life in the house for a while will cheer me up until my nephew arrives tomorrow. He'll be staying with me for a couple of weeks, and I'm so looking forward to it, but it's made the empty house that much harder to bear these past few days."

Lorelei knew she couldn't say no to *that*, so she reluctantly agreed. She hesitated before she left, though, and said, "Are you feeling okay? Other than the loneliness, I mean."

"Right as rain, dear," the older woman said with a smile. "Thank you, Lorelei. She'll be wonderful company, and my night is looking much more cheerful now."

With one last, reluctant glance at Latte, Lorelei nodded and walked away, trying to put Mr. Bath's words out of her head.

CHAPTER THREE

Lorelei slept fitfully that night, though whether it was the slightly off chicken she had taken a chance on or Latte's absence, she didn't know. It was during one of her more awake moments, when she surfaced from sleep to kick the tangled blankets off her legs, that she noticed the flashing blue and red lights illuminating her ceiling. For a dizzy moment, she thought she was in her old college apartment again, and that the lights from the bar across the street had begun to strobe for some reason.

Then she remembered that she was almost a decade older than the naive college graduate she had been and was in her own home on the quiet Honey Bee

Street in Wildborne, where nothing ever happened, and she sat up with a jolt.

Police lights. Had she slept through the sirens, or had there not been any? She didn't know, and it didn't matter. The vague bad feeling that had gripped her ever since she left Latte with Mrs. Whittaker returned full force, and she hurried over to her bedroom window, which looked out over the older woman's house.

The sight of four police cruisers with their lights on parked in the driveway and along the curb didn't surprise her, but it did make her stomach twist violently, and she gripped the windowsill tightly to keep from being sick. Focusing, she forced herself to take slow, deep breaths. *I don't know what happened,* she reminded herself. *She might be perfectly fine.* The police cruisers — the entirety of Wildborne's force, she knew — belied her hope, but she clung to it stubbornly, nonetheless.

As soon as she felt a bit more like herself, she hurried downstairs, her bare feet slapping against the wooden floorboards as she ran. She skidded to a stop by the kitchen door and unlocked it with shaking hands, not bothering to put on her sandals before she rushed outside.

The night was warm, and the humidity seemed to press down around her like a blanket. It was silent, without even the usually never-ending crickets making a noise, other than for the low murmur of voices coming from the people gathered in front of Mrs. Whittaker's house. She slowed down to a walk as she crossed the yard, her bare feet moving quietly across the cool, damp grass. She wondered if this was a dream. It felt like a dream.

Then a loud, brash voice called out, "Lorelei!" and she knew it wasn't a dream, because she would never dream about Marigold, bad chicken or no.

Marigold was standing near one of the police cruisers and had somehow managed to spot Lorelei in the dark. She was now waving her over, which caused all four of the police officers to turn and look at her as one. Lorelei barely noticed this, though, because Marigold had stepped into the spill of the cruiser's headlights, and the front of her pajamas and her sleeves were covered in blood.

Lorelei had never fainted before in her life, but it was

a close thing this time. Luckily, one of the officers came over to her and managed to catch her arm just as she stumbled. "There, there," he said, which she had never actually heard anyone say before in real life. It was enough to bring her brain solidly back to reality, where it anchored itself in her skull and caused the world to stop spinning.

"Miss? Are you okay?"

"What happened?" she asked, gaping at Marigold.

"Oh, it was just terrible, Lorelei," the other woman began. "I tried to help her, but it was too late. She was already gone when I got here."

"Gone? Gone where?" She wondered if Mrs. Whittaker had gone to the hospital, though some part of her was whispering that that was wrong. She knew what Marigold meant, but it took her neighbor spelling it out for her to admit it to herself.

"She's dead, Lorelei."

She shook her head, feeling the urge to run back to her house, where she might wake up in the morning to discover that this had all been a bad dream, but the officer's grip on her arm tightened and she knew she was trapped there.

"What happened?"

"That's what we're trying to figure out," he said grimly. "Did you hear anything strange tonight, ma'am?"

"No. I had no idea anything was wrong until I saw the lights." She nodded at the police vehicles. "Did she have a-a stroke or something?" As soon as she said it, she knew she was being dense. Of course, Mrs. Whittaker hadn't had a stroke. A stroke wouldn't explain all of the blood on Marigold.

"She was attacked in her home," he said, releasing her arm at last. "Did you notice anyone unusual in the neighborhood during the day, or any strange vehicles parked along the street this past week?"

"No," she said again. "Are you saying someone killed her? Who would want to do that?"

"That's what we're trying to figure out. Can I have your name, please?"

"Lorelei French. But why—"

"Lorelei, isn't that your cat?"

She jolted at Marigold's voice, which was very loud and very close. It wasn't difficult to follow the pointing finger to a crouched figure in the bushes. Latte's green eyes were reflecting the headlights from the police vehicles.

"Latte!"

At the sound of her name, the cat darted out of the bushes and over to Lorelei, who bent over and scooped her up. The cat was purring so much that her entire body seemed to vibrate, as she lay happily in her owner's arms.

The officer watched this with a bemused look on his face. "If that's all, Ms. French, you can—"

"Hold on," Marigold said, interrupting again. "She was talking to Mrs. Whittaker yesterday. I saw them. Maybe she told her something."

"You spoke to her yesterday too," Lorelei shot back. "Did you tell them about the flowers?"

"I told them Mrs. Whittaker and I had a perfectly civil discussion in which she agreed to move her flowers," Marigold said with a sniff.

"That's not what happened. She said she couldn't—"

"Ladies," the officer interrupted. "I hate to interrupt, but is any of this significant? By which I mean, did your neighbor say or do anything out of the ordinary, or that made you think she might be in some sort of trouble?"

"No," Marigold said shortly.

Lorelei was about to say the same thing, then remembered something the older woman had said. "Her nephew was supposed to come to visit tomorrow. Or today, I guess, if it's past midnight. Someone should tell him what happened."

Her voice cracked on the last word and she took a deep breath. She was not going to lose it, not in front of Marigold and the police officers. That could wait for when she was inside, where only Latte could see her.

"We'll make sure someone calls him," the officer said. "Thank you, Ms. French. You're free to go back to your home now. If you remember anything else that might be of help, give the station a call. And Ms. Marsters, can you go with Officer Bigly? She'll take you into your home and provide an evidence bag for your clothes, so you can finally change."

Lorelei turned away but glanced back as she walked toward her house. She saw a female police officer approach Marigold and guide her gently toward her house. Marigold shot a look toward Mrs. Whittaker's house, but the shadows cast by the light from the police cruisers made it impossible to see her face.

Once inside, Lorelei shut and locked the kitchen door behind her then, still clutching Latte, she sank down to the floor and started to cry. Mrs. Whittaker was dead. Mrs. Whittaker, who had baked her muffins and scones every Sunday morning and lent her advice about her garden every spring. And it was all her fault. Hadn't Mr. Bath told her that Latte always knew when someone was about to die? He had said she stuck to the residents like glue and the evening before, Latte had been so adamant about staying with Mrs. Whittaker that she had even gone so far as to hiss at Lorelei. She'd felt the first beginnings of doubt then, but she had ignored it because she didn't want to sound crazy, and she had thought that if the older woman was going to die in her sleep, there would be nothing she could do anyway. Mr. Bath had never said that the deaths were preventable, and surely, they would have tried.

But she could have prevented *this*. If she had been there, or if she had kept a watch on Mrs. Whittaker's house overnight, she might have been able to stop the attack. She knew that, while her fingerprints weren't on any murder weapon, Mrs. Whittaker's death was just as much her fault as if she had killed her herself.

CHAPTER FOUR

Her alarm went off a few hours later, and the lack of sleep made her feel numb and clumsy as she got ready for work. Despite how exhausted she felt, both in body and in mind, she didn't even consider not going in to work. People were depending on her for their morning jolt of energy. Besides, chances were that any of her employees she might call to cover for her were still sound asleep.

With some effort, she got Latte into her carrier after a hurried breakfast for the cat and managed to pull out of the driveway only a few minutes behind her normal schedule. She determinedly did not look at Mrs. Whittaker's house as she drove past.

The drive to French Roast had never felt so long, but

at last she pulled into the familiar parking lot, lit by the dawn's early light and a single, orange streetlamp. Once inside, she took Latte up front and opened the carrier. The cat stretched, then jumped up onto the bed on the window seat, where she could watch the comings and goings outside. Lorelei took a moment to go over the front room again to make sure she and Alyssa hadn't missed anything the day before, then went into the back.

The kitchen was her comfort zone. While she could prepare most drinks up front, back here was where she did her baking and where she made the smoothies and protein shakes. French Roast specialized in coffee, but it also served everything from tea to freshly baked cinnamon rolls. She drew the line just after baked goods, though. She had a hard enough time keeping up with the widely varied coffee demands to even think about stocking lunch meats and cheeses. Her customers could order a bagel, but if they wanted anything other than cream cheese on it, they were out of luck.

She reached for a container of fresh blueberries, meaning to make scones, but stopped before she touched the box, something that felt like a vise clutching her heart. Her scone recipe was from Mrs.

Whittaker. No, she would make croissants instead this morning. There were always the blueberry bagels that got delivered fresh every day from the bakery down the street, if her customers wanted something on the sweet side.

She was halfway through making the croissants when one of her employees, Henry Lockwood, came in through the back door. He blinked up at her, giving her a tired smile, before wordlessly going over to the week's printed out schedule to write down the time he had arrived.

"Good morning," he said once he was done neatly writing the numbers down. "Just starting on the food?"

She made a face but aimed it at the half-mixed croissant dough instead of at him. Henry was her oldest employee, age wise, and wasn't quite as receptive to the sarcasm she and her other employees enjoyed. He always took things too seriously, and she ended up feeling bad.

"Yes, I had a late start this morning. Can you get the iced tea ready? It looks like it will be a hot one."

"The whole summer has been a hot one," he grumbled, but he got the pitcher out and started measuring out water.

They worked in peaceful silence. One of her favorite things about Henry was how well he did his work without any complaint or prodding. She figured it was the sort of life skill that most people learned after sixty-five years, especially someone like Henry, who had worked with his hands his entire life. She still wasn't quite sure why he had chosen to work at French Roast, of all places. She knew he wanted something to keep him busy after his wife passed, but the careful attention he gave to each and every drink he made had come as a pleasant surprise. He may not have been what most people envisioned when they thought of someone who worked at a coffee shop, but he could make a mean mocha.

Once the first batch of croissants were in the oven, she turned on two large coffee makers for her house variety of real and decaf, which were both self-serve. The espresso and more expensive variants of coffee were made as they were ordered, along with the hot tea she offered. All that was left was to put the morning's bagels out on display, which was a good thing, since she was still running a few minutes behind. She usually gave herself some extra time in the mornings, but she was racing against the clock today.

She turned the open sign over one minute past seven, and there was already a line outside her door. These were her regulars, and she put on a brave face for them.

"Good morning," she said cheerily. "We've got croissants, hot and just out of the oven, and the house coffee is brewing as we speak."

There wasn't much chatter this early in the morning, for which she was glad. The smile felt strained on her face, and by the time the first rush of customers who were in a hurry to get to work left, she had a pounding headache, most likely from the lack of sleep. There was a short lull after the work rush, and she took the opportunity to make herself a vanilla latte, which she sipped as she tidied up behind the counter.

She had just enough time to feel the caffeine start to kick in before the next set of customers walked through the doors. She recognized one of them, a local named Walker Green. He had applied for a job at the coffee shop a while ago; she thought she still had his application somewhere. She didn't have a particularly high turnover rate of employees, though, and hopefully wouldn't have an opening for a while. She liked her current team. There was a lot to be said about working someplace where everyone got along, without the workplace drama she had experienced in some of her earlier jobs.

"Hey, Walker," she said as he approached the counter. "What will it be today?"

"Just black coffee for me," he said.

She nodded and reached for a mug, which she handed over to him so he could fill it at the self-serve station himself. It had taken her a while, but eventually she realized that she could tell his current status of employment by what he ordered. When he had a steady job, he got the more expensive lattes and cappuccinos. When he was out of work, he always just ordered black coffee. In a town as small as Wildborne, employment opportunities could be few and far apart, especially for people who didn't have a trade or a degree. She liked him well enough, and was sometimes tempted to hire him part time just so he could have something to fall back on when one of his other jobs fell through, but it wouldn't be fair to her other employees, who all needed the hours they had.

"And what can I get you?" she asked, turning her attention to his companion, who she didn't recognize. He was about the same age as Walker — early twenties, she estimated — but she guessed he wasn't a local. The flashy car she could see parked along the road in front of the coffee shop definitely wasn't one she had seen around town.

"Um…" He looked at the menu and his gaze turned blank as he took in all of their options. After a moment, he shook himself. "Can I have the white chocolate mocha? That sounds good."

"You won't regret it, man," Walker said. "I told you, this place has the best coffee of anywhere you've ever been."

The other young man didn't quite look like he believed it, but he politely accepted the mocha from Lorelei when she handed it over. She took great joy in watching his face go from somewhat skeptical to shocked as he sipped it.

"This is great," he said. "Do you have stores elsewhere?"

"Nope. This is the one and only French Roast."

Walker finished getting his coffee and slid onto one of the stools in front of the small bar set up on the front counter, shooting his friend an 'I told you so' look. "Eddie here is from out of town," he said. "He seemed to think Wildborne didn't have anything to offer but some trees and no stoplight."

"There's a stop sign," Lorelei pointed out, feeling the urge to defend her town. "And a committee has been trying to get a light installed." She shook her head realizing she was getting distracted. "Anyway, welcome to town… Eddie, was it?"

"Edward Bailey," he said, putting his coffee down to shake her hand. "And thanks. I'm honestly at a loss right now, so if I zone out don't be offended. I was supposed to be visiting my great-aunt, but she passed away last night. I think I'm still in shock. Walker had enough of me staring at the wall all morning and decided some caffeine and sugar might do me some good."

"Your… you don't mean Mrs. Whittaker, do you?" she asked.

"Did you know her?"

"Pretty much everybody knows everybody in Wildborne, but yes. She was my neighbor. I knew her well. I'm so sorry for your loss."

"Thank you. I just don't understand what happened. The police told me that she was murdered." He blinked down at his coffee. "My aunt was such a nice person. She practically raised my mom after my grandmother passed away. She's been a grandmother to me, and was always there when I needed something. I'm never going to forgive myself for not visiting her more. I should've come earlier — I should have stayed the whole week, and not waited until Friday to come. If I had been here, none of this would've happened."

"None of this is your fault," Lorelei said with feeling. "You had no way of knowing that she was in trouble. She was so excited about your visit, and I promise that she was happy during her last days. I had breakfast with her every Sunday, and I chatted with her almost every day. She loved her family, and she knew that you loved her too." She fell silent, wincing slightly when she remembered that she was talking with a complete stranger about a very sensitive matter. "I'm sorry if I'm overstepping. But she was a friend of mine, and I know she wouldn't want you to blame yourself for this."

"Thanks." He gave her a halfhearted smile. "I'm going to be in town until her funeral — Walker's letting me stay with him until then — and I hope you'll come. I'm not sure how all of the funeral preparations work, but if you need an invitation to go to one, consider yourself invited."

"Thank you," she said with feeling. "I'll be there. And if you need anything in the meantime, feel free to stop in here. Wildborne's got more to it than meets the eye."

CHAPTER FIVE

It wasn't until Lorelei was getting ready to leave for the day that she noticed the cat bed Latte usually occupied was empty. After spending almost twenty minutes looking around the coffee shop for her, even in the places Latte never went, like the kitchen, she had to admit defeat. *She must have slipped out the front door*, she thought. *She could be anywhere by now.*

She hurried to finish getting ready to go, and ran headlong into Henry as she entered the kitchen again. The coffee he was carrying spilled across her shirt, leaving a painfully hot mess that she knew from experience would dry to be unpleasantly sticky down her front. It was the final straw for her. The past twenty-four hours had been some of the worst of her life, and she just couldn't take it anymore.

Waving off Henry's apologies — she knew it wasn't his fault, but she still wanted to snap at someone, so she thought it was best to keep her mouth shut — she grabbed her purse, double checked to make sure she had her phone, and slipped out the back door. Mary would be in soon for the afternoon shift, and Henry could hold down the fort on his own for a few minutes. She desperately needed to get home and get changed, if only so she could go back out and start looking for her cat.

With a monumental effort of will, Lorelei ignored both Mrs. Whittaker's empty house and Latte's empty carrier when she got home. Instead, she made a beeline for the shower, where she got cleaned up, and then changed into fresh clothes. She took a moment to grab a few slices of deli meat from the fridge, which she ate quickly to tide her over, then went back outside, intending to drive into town and begin the search for her cat. She was waylaid when she saw a lonely figure standing in front of Mrs. Whittaker's house.

"Marigold?" she asked hesitantly, pausing partway to her car.

The other woman jumped, then spun to face her. "Lorelei. What are you doing?"

"Going out..." she said, gesturing haltingly at her car, feeling confused at the woman's accusing tone. "What are *you* doing?"

"Nothing," she snapped. She turned and started walking away, but Lorelei called after her.

"Marigold, wait! Can we talk?"

She watched as the other woman took another step away, then hesitated and reluctantly turned to face her. "What about?"

She took a deep breath. "I want to talk about what happened to Mrs. Whittaker. Last night was a jumble of confusion, and the police weren't really clear to me about what happened. But you were there before me. Do you know anything about it?"

For a moment, she thought her neighbor was going to ignore her and walk away anyway, but the urge to gossip proved to be too much. Marigold slunk closer, her eyes darting around as if watching out for eavesdroppers.

"I was in my kitchen and just happened to glance out the window in time to see a shadowy figure leave through her front door. The figure was running, and I thought it was strange — Mrs. Whittaker was too old to move like that. I came outside to see what was going on, but by then whoever it was, was gone. I happened to see that her front door was still open, though, and I decided to investigate. That's when I found her." Her eyes seemed to look past Lorelei now as she remembered the night before. "She was on the kitchen floor, and there was blood everywhere. I tried to stop the bleeding, but I think I was already too late. When I realized there wasn't anything I could do, I called the police. And you saw the rest."

"Did someone shoot her?"

Marigold shook her head. "I think she was stabbed. I remember seeing a knife on the floor. It was dark, though, and I didn't look too closely."

"I understand." Lorelei hesitated. "Thank you. For trying to help her. I know you didn't like her, and you didn't have to try to help her, but—"

"I didn't like her, true, but that doesn't mean I would have left her to die if I could help it," Marigold interrupted sharply. "I know you, and everyone on the block, think I'm some sort of nasty witch, but I'm not the sort to leave my neighbor bleeding out on the floor. You don't have to thank me for acting like a decent human being."

"I didn't mean it like that," Lorelei said weakly.

"There's a big distinction between not liking someone and wanting them dead, Lorelei. You should learn the difference."

With that, Marigold spun on her heel and stalked away, leaving Lorelei feeling even worse than she had when she began the conversation. With a sigh, she got into her car and pulled out of the driveway. Everything seemed to be spinning out of control. All she could do was pray that she could find Latte. She didn't think she could face the coming night completely alone in her house if she didn't.

CHAPTER SIX

Wildborne wasn't big, but it was sprawling. The hilly forests of Wisconsin made a compact, neatly laid out town impossible. Main Street and the intersecting, Forest Street, were the two main roads, but there was a maze of smaller streets sprouting off each. Lorelei wasn't sure where to begin her search. Latte was a smart cat, almost frighteningly so at times. She had never snuck out of the coffee shop before, and her gut told her that the cat had had a reason to do so this time. Determining the reason, however, seemed impossible. As smart as Latte was, she couldn't exactly leave her owner a note. *Though life would be a lot simpler if she did*, she thought as she drove slowly around the block that French Roast was on.

Lorelei's only comfort was that everyone in town knew whose cat Latte was. She was a regular fixture at French Roast, and her brown coat and green eyes were easily recognizable. She was also wearing a collar, a pretty silver thing with a tiny tag on it that had her name and Lorelei's cell phone number. All she could do was hope a person found her before the cat ran into one of the dangers of the wider world.

She drove around town, making slow circles around each block and occasionally pausing to get out of the car and call out Latte's name, for almost an hour before she finally spotted her. The mocha colored cat was following closely behind a man who looked to be about a decade older than Lorelei. He was walking quickly, occasionally glancing behind himself at the cat and, once, pausing to make shooing motions at her. The cat was not discouraged; if anything, she seemed to follow him even closer after that.

Lorelei was ready to brake and get out, but she hesitated. She could have prevented Mrs. Whittaker's death, if she had only trusted Latte and the strange warning Mr. Bath had given her about the cat. Was this another example of Latte knowing a person's fate? While friendly enough to strangers, especially if they complimented her suitably first, the cat wasn't prone to following them around like this. The only other time Lorelei had seen her so reluctant to leave someone's side was the night before.

She took her foot off the brake pedal and placed it on the gas pedal instead, speeding up from her crawl to pass the pair. As she drove by, she could have sworn that Latte looked right at her.

Spending her evening stalking a man and a cat on foot was not what Lorelei had planned when she woke up. Granted, she hadn't had *any* plans for the evening, besides maybe drinking a glass of wine and calling her mother to share her grief over Mrs. Whittaker's death, but if she'd had plans, this wouldn't have featured in them.

The man looked vaguely familiar, enough so that she knew she'd seen him around town before, but she couldn't come up with his name. All she had managed to learn in the past half-hour was that he liked to walk. A lot. They had made their way around several blocks, Lorelei staying far enough behind that she sometimes lost sight of him as he rounded a corner. He seemed to have gotten used to the cat following him, because he had stopped looking at her, and instead had put in a pair of earbuds and seemed to be listening to music. Lorelei wasn't in terrible shape, but she didn't spend as much time exercising as she probably should, and his fast pace was making her short of breath. By the time they looped back around to a block near the one they had started on, all she could do was be thankful that he wasn't a jogger.

The house he stopped at was only a short distance from where she had first seen him. She could see her car parked down the street and was glad to see that a few other people had parked their vehicles along the curb as well, so it no longer looked so out of place.

That didn't stop *her* from feeling out of place. She hung back awkwardly, a quarter of a block away, while the man unlocked the front door and went inside. As soon as he shut the door, she hurried closer and hid behind a large bush at the corner of his property. Now that his evening exercise seemed to be over and he was enclosed by four walls, Lorelei wasn't quite sure what to do. She was beginning to feel more than a bit foolish about the whole thing. What had she been thinking? That she would follow him for a while and then dart forward to keep him from stepping in front of a speeding car when he tried to cross the street without looking? Latte had spent hours with

Mrs. Whittaker before the attack, and from what Mr. Bath had told her, she had spent hours with each of the residents she had kept company with as well.

She eyed Latte, who had been left outside thanks to some quick, yet gentle, prodding by the man. The cat looked thoroughly offended and seemed to glare at the door for a long moment before letting out a plaintive meow. When no answer was forthcoming, she gave a louder meow, then began scratching at the door. After a moment, it opened, and the man poked his head out to frown down at her.

"What do you want?" he asked. There was irritation in his voice, but it was mild, and his gaze softened as he gazed down at Latte. "Look, you're cute and all, but you obviously have an owner already. And don't think I'm going to feed you. I know you won't ever leave if I do."

Latte just meowed again, sounding pitiful this time, and he sighed.

"Fine. You can come in, but only so I can look at your collar and see if that tag of yours has a phone number on it. Then you're going home. Are we clear?"

He stepped aside and Latte sauntered in, rubbing her

body against his calf and letting her tail curl around his leg as she went by. He looked down at her, shook his head, then shut the door firmly, leaving Lorelei completely stumped as to what to do next.

She jumped a moment later when her cell phone rang. Pulling it out of her pocket, she frowned at the unfamiliar number on the screen, then winced when she realized who it probably was.

"Hello?"

"Hi. Is this the owner of a cat whose name is… Latte?"

"Yes, it's me," she said, biting back a groan. This whole evening was turning into one big mess.

"Well, your cat followed me on my daily walk and ended up coming home with me. I can give you my address, if you're available to come pick her up."

"Thank you. She went missing from my shop earlier today. I was worried about her." It was all true, at least; she hated lying, and always avoided it when she could.

He rambled off his address, which she pretended to take down, and she promised to be there in ten minutes. That would leave more than enough time for her to walk the short distance to her car, get in, and drive around for long enough that she could pretend she hadn't been watching the whole encounter from the bushes.

She thanked him and hung up, then hurried back to her car. It wasn't until she was standing next to the tiny convertible that she realized she had another problem. Her purse was sitting on the passenger seat. On top of the purse, were her keys. Without much hope, she tugged on the door handle. Locked.

She felt something suspiciously like tears prick her eyes, but blinked them away, chiding herself for being ridiculous. Yes, this had been the worst and longest twenty-four hours of her life. But she wasn't going to cry. Locking her keys in the car was *not* going to be what sent her over the edge. Not if she could help it.

She had her phone, at least, and thanks to Mrs. Whittaker, she knew that there was a local locksmith. Her neighbor had locked herself out a couple of times in the past few years before finally printing a spare for Lorelei to keep. She clearly remembered serving her tea before pulling her laptop out and searching for locksmiths. She even remembered the man's name, and a quick google search on her phone was enough to supply the business number of one Gerald Strauss.

It was embarrassing to explain her predicament, but he took it in good humor and promised he would be there shortly to let her into her car. By now, she only had a few minutes left before she was supposed to collect Latte, and she doubted he would arrive before then, so she hurried back over to the house her cat had disappeared into and, hoping that the man didn't notice her lack of a car or her disheveled appearance, knocked on the door.

It opened almost immediately, and she spotted an irate Latte clutched in his arms. He extended the cat toward her, an eyebrow raised.

"You're the one I called about the cat?"

"Yes," she said, taking Latte from him and ignoring the cat's growl. "Thank you for calling. I hope she wasn't too much trouble."

"Not at all. I'm glad to help her get back to you safely."

She smiled her goodbye at him and, keeping a tight

grip on Latte, walked back down the path to the sidewalk. The cat squirmed, but Lorelei didn't let her go.

"I know," she hissed. "You think something's going to happen to him. But unless you can stop it with your own four paws, you have to trust me. I want to try to save him. We'll keep an eye on him, I promise."

To her surprise, Latte stopped struggling. Lorelei didn't let her guard down completely, knowing how quickly cats could move when they put their minds to it, but she did relax somewhat. Latte had always acted smarter than the other cats she knew; it was possible she had at least somewhat understood her words, or at least the intent behind them.

She leaned against her car, the cat in her arms, while she waited for Gerald Strauss to arrive. When she saw an old truck puttering up the street, she straightened. It pulled to a stop behind her car, and a man with graying hair got out, eyeing her, the cat, and the car for a moment before grinning.

"I'm glad I hurried. That cat doesn't look thrilled."

"She's not," Lorelei said. "Thanks for coming. It's been a... difficult day, and this is just the icing on the cake."

"I'll get you sorted in no time," he said. He went around to the bed of his truck and took out something that looked like a sturdy wire with a hook on the end. All it took was a moment of jiggling, and he popped the driver's side door open. "These old cars don't have all of the modern security features. It makes life easier most of the time, though it makes things easier for car thieves too."

"Thank you," she said with feeling. She put Latte into the carrier on the small back seat, then extracted her wallet from her purse. After paying him — he asked for less than she thought was fair, considering how quickly he had come to her rescue — she wished him well and he tipped an imaginary hat to her, then went on his way.

Once she was safely ensconced in her car, she turned in her seat to look at Latte, who was sitting in the carrier, her tail flicking back and forth.

"I'm committing to this for one night only," she said. "And only because I don't want another death on my conscience. If you were just following him because he ate salmon for lunch or something, I'm going to be very annoyed. Understood?" The cat met her gaze evenly, and Lorelei sighed. "Fine. I'd better not get accused of being a stalker. A restraining order is the last thing I need."

She pulled away from the curb and headed back into town, stopping at a gas station to grab a cold soda and a pre-made sandwich for herself, and a can of generic cat food for Latte. The cat was used to the higher-end food the pet shop the next town over sold, but she would have to deal with it for now. Lorelei didn't want to be away from the man's house — she still hadn't gotten his name; it was a sign of how much at the end of her rope she was that she hadn't thought to ask — for any longer than necessary, but if she was planning a stakeout, she knew she needed some sort of refreshment. The caffeine in the soda wouldn't go amiss either.

When she returned, she parked on a different side of the street from before, and was closer to the house, to make it easier to keep an eye on the man as best she could. She knew it wasn't the best plan. After all, if he tripped and fell down the stairs or something, she wouldn't even know, let alone be able to save him from his fate. All she could do was hope that she would notice *something* in time to help him. *Maybe Latte will get my attention somehow*, she thought, glancing back at the cat, who was ignoring the can of food and was staring directly at the house, nothing moving but the tip of her tail. Deciding that if they were going to be there for a while, the cat might as well have her freedom, she opened the carrier's door. Latte came out and jumped onto the dashboard, draping herself across it so she could gaze at the house in comfort.

The sun dipped behind the trees slowly, and the soft glow of evening became the grey of twilight. Lorelei dozed; she woke up before six every morning in order to open the coffee shop at seven, and she hadn't gotten more than a few hours of sleep the night before. It was hard to stay focused in the warm car, even with the windows cracked, and the soda didn't help her as much as she had hoped. It wasn't until Latte gave a loud meow that she jerked awake to see the cat standing on her rear feet, front paws bracing against the passenger side windowsill as she stared out the window, and she realized with a surge of fear that something was very wrong.

It was full dark out now, and the windows of every house were black. Every house except for one. In the front window of the house she was supposed to be watching, the flickering orange light of an open flame was slowly growing brighter.

CHAPTER SEVEN

Lorelei yanked the driver's side door open and tumbled out, trying not to step on Latte, who darted out around her like a bolt of lightning. Pausing only long enough to cast a look both ways down the road, she crossed the street, following the cat, who quickly disappeared into the shadows.

She made for the front door, taking the porch steps in one bound, and reached for the door handle, only to find it both warm and locked. Mentally berating herself for her stupidity - the fire looked like it was in the room the door opened up to - she hurried around to the side of the house instead.

Indecision made her jittery. She has left her phone in

the car in her panic, and she didn't want to waste time going back to get it, but she didn't know what else she could do. Had he left a back door unlocked, maybe? But what would she do when she got inside? If he was hurt, she didn't know if she was strong enough to drag him out.

She was about to run to a neighbor's house and pound on their door, begging for help, when she heard a yowl from further down the side of the house. She squinted, and saw the dark shape of a cat, pawing at the siding under a window. Deciding that she had trusted Latte this far, and might as well do it a while longer, she hurried over to the cat and peered into the window. It was dark, and the air was hazy from the fire in the other room, but she could make out the shape of a bed with someone on it.

"Hey!" she shouted, pounding on the window. "Wake up!"

There was no response from the person on the bed. She tried to remember how long it took someone to suffer from smoke inhalation, but if she had ever known that information, it had long since vanished, along with other miscellanea such as how to do advanced calculus.

She half turned, trying to decide which house to run to for help, when Latte meowed again, forcing her attention back to the window. The cat's eyes reflected the scant starlight, and Lorelei had the strangest feeling the cat was waiting for her to do something.

"You don't want him to die either, do you?" she muttered.

Refocusing on the window, she decided to try her luck. She managed to pry the screen off easily enough, then she braced her hands against the glass and pushed upwards. It opened, letting out a warm gust of acrid, smoky air.

She shouted again, but the person on the bed still didn't move. Before her sense of self-preservation could kick in, she jumped and leveraged herself in through the window, wincing as the sill bit into her stomach. Knowing she would have bruises and scrapes in the morning, she awkwardly swung her leg around and half fell onto the bedroom floor.

She was up in an instant and hurried over to the bed, where she shook the still form of the man who had been kind enough to call her about Latte. When he groaned and turned over, she felt as though she could cry from relief.

"Come on, get up, get up," she said, giving up on shaking him and resorting to dumping the half-full glass of water on his bedside table over his face.

He sat up, spluttering, then gaped at her. She knew that waking up to find a strange woman standing over his bed and a room full of smoke had to be disconcerting, but she didn't have any time to ease him into it. The smoke was making her eyes sting, and she could hear a distinct roaring. The fire had grown in just the few minutes since she had last seen it.

"Your house is on fire," she said. "We have to get out, now."

He still seemed out of it, but he leveraged himself to his feet and followed her to the windowsill. She climbed through on her own, then turned to help him out, supporting him when he stumbled.

"Does anyone else live with you? Do you have any pets?"

"N-no," he managed, staring at his house in shock.

She breathed a sigh of relief. She really didn't want to have to go in there again.

"I need to go get my phone. Someone has to call the fire department before the whole place burns down."

She turned to go back to her car, intending to leave him momentarily while Latte rubbed against his ankles, but he reached out and snagged her arm. "Wait. You... you saved my life. I take sleeping medication. I wouldn't have woken up on my own."

She felt a surge of... something... at the sight of the pure gratefulness in his eyes. It hadn't really struck her until this moment; without her, he would have died. Because of what she had done, as odd and insane as it had all seemed at the time, he was still alive, and would hopefully get to live decades that he wouldn't have otherwise. It was a good feeling. One of the best feelings she had ever had, in fact. Though, it wasn't all due to her. She managed to shoot him a quick smile.

"Don't thank me. Thank the cat."

. . .

Lorelei stumbled into her own bed two hours later, her skin still damp from the shower she had taken to wash the smoke smell off. It still seemed to cling to her hair, but she could figure that out in the morning. Latte was already curled up in the middle of the bed, seemingly dead to the world. She didn't blame her; sleeping for the next two days straight seemed like a tempting plan just about now.

She fell into bed, curling her body awkwardly around the cat, and let unconsciousness take her. When her alarm went off, she woke up just enough to call Jenny, who was on the schedule for the afternoon shift, and beg her to take the morning one instead. As soon as she heard the somewhat worried agreement from the other woman, she ended the call and let sleep reclaim her.

When she woke again, it was after ten in the morning. She hadn't slept that late in years, but she also hadn't had such an insane day before — ever. She took another shower in an attempt to get the last of the smoke smell from her hair, then sat down at her tiny kitchen table by the window and gazed out at the street while Latte ate her breakfast. She had a few hours before she had to go in to work, and she had a lot to think about.

She had saved the man, whose name she had finally learned. He was Terrance Stanford, a single father with two adult children, who worked at a local insurance company. He lived a perfectly normal, happy life, and had people who loved him and depended on him. The thought of the grief they would all be feeling right now if she had failed made her heart feel like it was shriveling.

She had been skeptical before. It wasn't that she had completely disregarded everything Mr. Bath had told her, but believing that her cat somehow knew when someone was about to die, was a big leap to make on faith alone. Now, however, she had no doubts. Latte had stuck to both Mrs. Whitaker and Mr. Stanford like glue the day preceding their fatal encounters — or nearly fatal, in Mr. Stanford's case. Lorelei had dropped the ball horribly when it came to Mrs. Whitaker, but now she had proven to herself that she could affect people's fates — if fate was even the right word. Was it fate when it was avoidable?

And perhaps even more importantly, was it her duty to try saving others in the future? She didn't know if there was a philosophical answer to that, but she did know that her own moral compass wouldn't let her ignore it when people were in danger. She knew that, no matter how tired she might be after a long day at work or how stressed she might be, the second Latte disappeared again and decided to glue herself to some random stranger, she would be right there, trying to help. She couldn't just let people die.

It was a heavy weight to carry, though. She knew she'd had an easy life so far. Yes, she'd gone through her fair share of heartbreaks and loss, but nothing beyond what most people experienced. This… it was something else. It would be like being a superhero. A superhero with no powers and no secret identity, and a cat that was too smart for her own good.

She steeled herself, sitting up straighter and giving a firm nod, even though no one was there to see it. If she was going to resign herself to gallivanting around town, chasing behind Latte and saving lives, she wasn't going to waste time feeling bad for herself or complaining about it. She was just going to do it, and do it well.

Her phone's cheerful ringtone brought her back to the current moment, and she jumped up to grab it off the counter. Seeing her mother's name on the caller ID, she made a face, but answered it.

"Hey," she said, striving to sound casual.

"Hello, Lorelei. I was just calling to double check that you were still planning on visiting next weekend. I'm thinking of making a roast, but I won't bother if it's only going to be me."

"No, I'll come for the night like I said I would," she said. "The roast sounds good. You know, you could always visit me. I've got a guest room, and I'm much better at cooking now. No more ramen."

"It's not your house or the cooking that's the problem. You know that," her mother replied. "Do you still have the cat?"

Lorelei sighed. "You know I do."

"Well, you have your answer."

She bit her lip, fighting back the urge to bring up the old argument. Her mother hadn't visited her in six months, not since her grandmother's funeral, when Lorelei mentioned she was going to bring Latte home with her. It wasn't that her mother didn't like cats, or was allergic to them; they had even had cats when Lorelei was a child. But her mother refused to even be in the same room as Latte, and it wasn't until she and her mother had had a heart to heart over a couple of glasses of wine a few months ago that Lorelei had found out why. One of the staff members at the nursing home had let something slip about Latte's unusual ability, and her mother — her no-nonsense, what-you-see-is-what-you-get mother — had for some unfathomable reason believed the rumor wholeheartedly. Unlike Lorelei, she was convinced that Latte didn't just know when someone was about to die, but that she caused it.

It was a major piece of contention between them. Lorelei suspected that her mother somehow blamed the cat for her grandmother's death, and in a vague sort of way she could understand it. Her mother had taken the older woman's loss hard, and having a scapegoat likely made the loss easier to understand. But it was something neither of them would budge on; Lorelei wasn't about to get rid of Latte, and her mother didn't want to be near what she called the devil cat. It strained their relationship, but didn't break it, and a truce came in the form of Lorelei's one-sided visits to her mother and the understanding that Latte would never be a major conversation piece between them.

It meant that she could never share the newest part of her life with her mother, which hurt, but she could live with the secret. She'd have to.

CHAPTER EIGHT

She got to the coffee shop in time for the afternoon shift, armed with a can of Jenny's favorite energy drink. She felt horribly guilty about calling her employee into work on such short notice and wanted to make sure she knew she was appreciated. Still, she couldn't quite bring herself to regret doing it. She felt much better now that she had finally caught up on sleep.

Jenny took the drink with a grin of thanks, brushing a stray strand of her blonde hair behind her ear before tucking the drink into her purse. "I appreciate it, but you really didn't have to."

"And you didn't have to agree to come in, so we're even," Lorelei said with a smile. "Was it very busy?"

"About normal for the morning," she said. "Someone dropped their coffee; Henry is up front cleaning it now. Oh, and someone came in looking for you."

"Who?"

"Some guy," Jenny said, shrugging. "He didn't give his name; he left before I could ask for it."

"Well, thanks for telling me. Did you let him know I'll be in this afternoon?"

"I did. He said he'd be back."

Lorelei raised an eyebrow. That sounded a bit ominous.

"Well, I'd better be going," her employee continued. "I had some shopping I was going to do this morning, but it got put off, so I'd better get to it now. Have a good day. I hope you're feeling better."

She said goodbye to the younger woman and watched as she left, then put on her apron and her name tag. Henry came back into the kitchen, his hands full of soaking wet rags. He gave her a nod in greeting before dumping them in the basket that contained the laundry.

"You feeling all right?"

She nodded. "I am. I just needed the extra sleep. The past couple of nights have been... a bit insane."

"Life does that sometimes," he said with a chuckle.

She smiled, glad that he was there. Henry worked only three days a week, but usually stayed an hour or two into the afternoon shift, making the days he did work even longer than hers. He was retired and wanted the rest of the week free so he could pursue new hobbies, for which she couldn't blame him, though she often found herself wishing he could work more. He was a good, steady person to have around during the day, and never seemed to get flustered during the early rush. The shop got less busy in the afternoon, so usually one employee could close on their own. Mornings, on the other hand, were another beast entirely.

She stepped into the front and began taking orders, laughing and smiling with the customers. She felt as if weeks had passed since Mrs. Whitaker's death, instead of less than forty-eight hours. So much had happened between then and now that she felt almost like a different person entirely.

A couple of hours into her shift, a familiar and welcome face walked into the coffee shop. She beamed at the man she had saved and, as soon as her register was clear, waved him over. "Mr. Stanford, I'm glad to see you. How are you doing?"

"You should call me Terrence," he said. "And I'm doing well. A lot better than I'd be without you. I came here to check on you, and to thank you. I really owe you a lot."

She shook her head. "You don't owe me anything. I just did what anyone would have done."

"I'm not sure that's true, but regardless. I got something for you." He held up a bag she hadn't noticed when he came in and passed it over to her.

"What is it?" she asked. He raised an eyebrow, looking at the bag pointedly, and she fought back her questions and decided to just open it. She unwrapped the parcel, squinted at it for a moment, confused, then grinned widely. "This is perfect. You have no idea just how perfect it is. I still feel like I shouldn't accept it though…"

"Please, I really wanted to do something to show you how grateful I am. And I figured you might want a way to keep tabs on that cat if she gets out again."

Lorelei looked back down at the pet GPS tracker he had given her, knowing logically that she should try to refuse again, but she couldn't bring herself to do it. Just hours ago, she had decided to throw herself into this whole saving people thing headfirst, and now here was a way to keep track of Latte when she slipped out.

"I know you're working; I just wanted to give you that and thank you again."

"Wait," she said as he began to walk away. "I've been wondering... Did you find out yet what caused the fire?"

"They're still investigating it, but the firefighter I talked to said that it had the hallmarks of an electrical fire. Some of my wiring likely went bad, which was what started it."

"Oh, I see," she said, feeling a rush of relief. She had wondered, for a bit, if maybe something she or Latte had done had inadvertently caused the fire. She wasn't sure how all of this worked, and it wouldn't exactly be all that helpful if her presence was what ended up causing people to need help. "I guess it could have happened to anyone."

"It could," he said. "So, make sure your fire alarms have batteries in them. I'm definitely going to be upping my fire safety habits in the future. This was too close a call."

They said their goodbyes and he left, leaving Lorelei to smile happily at the box in her hands. She had left Latte home for the day, not quite emotionally prepared to deal with the cat's sneaking out again, but now she wouldn't have to worry about it. No matter where Latte went, she would be able to find her.

The door opened again while she was examining the GPS tracker, letting in another set of familiar faces. She looked up with a smile, putting the box to the side. This was turning out to be quite the busy afternoon, not in a business sense, but in a social one.

"Welcome to French Roast," she said as Mrs. Whitaker's nephew, Eddie, approached the counter, his friend beside him.

"Thanks," he said. He returned her smile faintly, then eyed the menu. He and his friend, Walker, made their orders and Lorelei began getting them ready. While she worked, Edward talked.

"The plans for my aunt's funeral were finalized, and I wanted to let you know that it's going to be next Wednesday. Will you be able to make it?"

"I will," she said, already mentally rearranging her schedule for the day. "Do you know what time?"

"Three in the afternoon."

"Okay, I'll be there." She would have to find someone to cover the last hour or so of her shift, but that shouldn't be too hard. "I know I said it already, but I'm really sorry for your loss," she added as she handed his coffee over.

"I just wish the police would find whoever killed her," he said. "Knowing that there are people out there who did that to her and that they're just getting away with it is hard. The police said there was no sign of forced entry, so that means that whoever killed her must have known her well enough that she let them in, or that they knew about her spare key. That makes it worse, somehow; I can't imagine how anyone who knew her would be willing to end her life."

"She wouldn't want you to be so preoccupied with it," Walker said, clapping him on the shoulder. "The police may not ever find them, I'm sure they don't get much practice with murders around here."

"You're supposed to be my supportive friend," Eddie said, rolling his eyes. "Telling me to just give up isn't exactly helping."

"I'm not saying give up," Walker said. "I'm just saying maybe brace yourself for it. I don't want to see you wasting away waiting for the killer to be found. You got a life to live. Oh, and I got the coffees." He nudged Eddie aside and took his wallet out, laying some bills on the counter. He told Lorelei to keep the change, for which she thanked him, and returned to his conversation with Edward. Not wanting to listen in now that the two were just talking among themselves, Lorelei moved away a bit. Another couple of customers walked in over the next few minutes, and she got them their coffee to go. They left with thanks and she smiled back warmly. She really did love her job. Just being here let her almost forget everything else that was going on in her increasingly crazy life.

CHAPTER NINE

When she got home that afternoon, she clipped the small GPS device onto Latte's collar. She made sure that the tracker was synced with the app on her phone that would let her see the cat's location on a map. When she got it to work, she grinned with triumph. The box held a second device, which she put in her purse in case Latte managed to lose the first one. The cat gazed at her in irritation when Lorelei looked down at her, sitting back to scratch at the collar before shaking her body like a wet dog.

"I'm sorry, I know it's a bit heavier than what you're used to, but it's really important, Latte. With this, we're going to be able to help a lot of people."

She felt a pang of guilt that was slowly becoming

familiar as she thought of Mrs. Whittaker. She wished so much that she had tried to save the older woman. The fact that she had been murdered, and hadn't just died in some horrible accident, made it worse. She remembered what Eddie had said at the coffee shop and agreed with it; the people or person who had killed her deserved to face justice.

She frowned. In a way, Mrs. Whittaker's death was her fault, though she knew that other people probably wouldn't agree. Did that mean it was also her job to solve the crime? She wouldn't even know where to begin, but then again, she did know almost everyone in town enough to recognize their faces, at least, and she knew chances were the killer was local. It wouldn't make sense for a visitor to kill Mrs. Whittaker for no reason. She had watched enough crime shows to know that people almost always had a motive for murder, whether that was greed, or revenge, or scorned love.

Moving over to the kitchen window, she looked out at Mrs. Whittaker's house. It was empty, and the crime scene tape was still up, but there were no police vehicles in front of it. If she just had a poke around, she might be able to find something that would help lead her to the killers, then she could anonymously give that information to the police. She knew they could do their own jobs, but they hadn't visited the older woman every week for years. She had. She would be in a better position to know if something was out of place.

She glanced over at Latte, narrowing her eyes. The cat had known Mrs. Whittaker was about to die, and she had been the only witness to the murder. Would she be able to help solve the crime? Lorelei felt a bit foolish for even thinking it, but then, Latte wasn't like other cats.

"Do you want to go over to Mrs. Whittaker's with me?" she asked the cat, who was still pawing at the new addition to her collar. Latte looked up at her, her expression giving nothing away. Biting her lip, Lorelei retrieved Mrs. Whittaker's key from on top of her fridge and scooped the cat up into her arms. She slipped out the front door and, trying not to look suspicious, strode across the yard to Mrs. Whittaker's house, where she stepped around a shattered plant pot and gently moved the crime scene tape aside to unlock the front door.

She stepped inside and immediately looked away from the mess on the floor. It struck her, suddenly, that she was standing only feet away from the very spot her friend had died. She fought back a shiver and looked around the room, trying to dredge up enough curiosity to keep her going.

She had seen the inside of Mrs. Whittaker's house plenty of times before. It was cluttered, with a lot of little knick-knacks, but everything always had its place. She had never seen it like this before, with all of the older woman's possessions strewn around as if a tornado had blown through. She walked slowly through the house, careful not to touch anything as she kept her eyes peeled for something that might tell her who the killer was, or at least what they wanted. It wasn't until she reached the older woman's bedroom that she found it – Mrs. Whittaker had a lovely, ornately carved jewelry box that sat on her vanity. Now, however, it was tipped over and empty, not a single piece of jewelry to be seen. She frowned, beginning to poke around the house with a bit more direction, and realized that all of Mrs. Whittaker's best items were gone; her good silverware, the jewelry, and even the lovely crystal glasses Lorelei had seen but never used. One of them was shattered on the floor, but the rest seemed to have made it out of the house safely.

When she heard the sound of a car slowing down, she jumped and ran back to the front of the house to look out the window, but it was just the mailman. Biting back a sigh of relief, she waited until the truck had moved on, then stepped out of the house, careful to lock it behind her. She glanced down at the shattered potted plant, something about it bothering her, then shook her head. Everything about this bothered her. Someone had killed Mrs. Whittaker, and now she had an idea why.

CHAPTER TEN

As she turned away from the house, two things happened at once. Latte, who was still in her arms after having made no indication of anything bothering her at the house, squirmed suddenly and leapt away from her, claws digging into Lorelei's stomach and arm as she jumped to the ground. Lorelei made an aborted grab for her, but a shouted, "Hey!" distracted her.

She spun, almost losing her balance at the sudden change in direction, to see Marigold striding across her yard toward her. The other woman was glaring at her, her face a mask of anger.

"What were you snooping around in there for?"

Lorelei winced, frantically trying to come up with a good reason other than that she was trying to figure out what killed the older woman. She didn't think Marigold would appreciate her trying her hand at amateur detective work. "I just… I was trying to…"

"Were you returning to the scene of the crime? Did you kill her?"

Lorelei blinked, jerking back and sputtering with both offense and befuddlement. "What? Me? Mrs. Whittaker was my friend. Why would I want to hurt her?"

"You're an odd one, Lorelei French. I don't know what goes on in that head of yours. There's no good reason for you to be snooping around the crime scene, none at all."

"You're right," Lorelei said. She raised her hands. "I'm sorry. I shouldn't have been in there. I just… I wanted some answers." She decided that honesty was probably the best way to go now, in the face of Marigold's glare.

"Answers?" the older woman asked, her eyes narrowing.

"I want to know who killed her and why."

"You think you're going to find answers the police can't?" Marigold scoffed. "I should report you, that's what I should do."

"Please don't," Lorelei said. When Marigold looked hesitant, she added, "I can tell you what I found."

As she'd hoped, the promise of gossip that she didn't even have to snoop around for seemed to make up Marigold's mind. "All right, hurry up with it."

"Someone robbed her," Lorelei said. "All of her valuables were gone. And according to her nephew, the police said there was no sign of forced entry. He thinks it was someone she knew."

Marigold's eyes narrowed in consideration. "So, it was a local. They're going to be sorry when the police find them."

"They are," Lorelei agreed. Mrs. Whittaker had been a kind soul, and everyone who met her liked her. People were going to be very upset when her killer was finally found.

"I really do have to go, though," she said. "I need to go get Latte."

"Don't let me see you in there again."

"I won't," she promised with a quick wave as she jogged off toward her house. Latte wasn't there, but her phone was, and she immediately opened the app. Latte had made it a decent distance down the block and seemed to be heading for the main part of town. Sighing, she gathered up her purse and her keys and went outside to get into her car, propping her phone up so she could see the screen while she drove.

She spotted Latte trotting on the sidewalk with determination that seemed rather un-catlike. She slowed the car down to a crawl, at a loss as to what to do next. She couldn't just scoop up the cat; that would defeat the whole purpose of the saving people thing she was trying to do. But how would she know when Latte got to where she was supposed to be? With a sigh, Lorelei pulled away, deciding to drive around and check back in with Latte as she progressed to wherever she was going. She ended up parking at a small park by the school, keeping an eye on her phone. About twenty minutes later, she noticed the cat's dot had stopped somewhere along Main Street, and she started her car again, heading for the area. If this kept up, she was going to have to start keeping books and some snacks in her car. Waiting with nothing to do except stare at her phone wasn't fun.

She saw Latte waiting outside of a shoe store and parked on the opposite side of the road. Taking the time to check both ways, she crossed the street, leaning against the wall a few yards away from the cat. Latte shot her an uninterested look, then continued staring at the door, A moment later, a man about her age came walking out, a shopping bag in his hand. He had dark brown hair that fell in gentle curls to his ears and a lanky frame. His face was attractive, with high cheekbones and eyes that seemed to be a light brown color from the glance she got of them behind his glasses.

Great, she thought. *I'm going to end up looking like a weirdo in front of an attractive stranger. I just love my life.*

He paused when he saw Latte and crouched down to pet her, then straightened up, walking down the street. Latte followed behind him, but he didn't seem to notice; the cat's footsteps were silent. Lorelei followed too, taking out her phone and pretending to talk on it in case he saw her.

He didn't; he seemed intent on getting wherever he was going; that is, until his own phone rang. He dug it out of his pocket, pressing it to his ear distractedly as he started to cross the street

Lorelei saw the old truck before he did. It was coming around the corner, and she could tell by the way the cars were parked along the street that the driver likely didn't see the man. The truck didn't slow down; in just seconds, the man Latte was following was going to step out in front of it.

Swearing, not having expected something to happen so quickly, Lorelei ran forward, almost tripping over Latte, who shot her an offended look, and managed to grab onto the man's arm. She yanked him back moments before the truck blew past, inches in front of his face. He dropped the shopping bag and phone, the latter falling to the street, getting crushed by the truck's tires.

He shouted in surprise and turned around, staring at her with wide eyes, looking back at the road, where the truck had blown past. It came to stop a little bit further down, and she spotted Gerald Strauss lean out the driver side window, glancing back at them with a worried look on his face. Lorelei jogged over to him, worried that he might have been hurt, after stopping so fast. "Is he all right? I didn't see you there."

"We're fine," Lorelei said. He seemed fine, just concerned. She spotted a box of what looked like glasses laying on its side in the passenger seat, but they were wrapped in bubble wrap, and it looked like they had survived as well. "No one got hurt." He nodded, his eyes still worried, but pulled his truck back into the street again.

She hurried back over to the man, who was still staring at her, eyes wide. "You just saved my life," he said.

She winced, realizing that she was going to be hearing those words a lot if she truly ended up being able to help people as much as she hoped she'd be able to. She glanced down, spotting Latte, who was sitting on the curb, grooming herself nonchalantly.

"I was just following my cat, who slipped away from me. It was pure luck that I saw the truck coming."

"Thank you," he said. He shook himself, some of the dazed look leaving his eyes, and stuck out his hand. "I'm Hugh. Hugh Howell."

"Lorelei French," she said, shaking his hand. She glanced down at the pieces of his phone. "Sorry about that."

"I'd rather the phone than the rest of me," he said. He bent down to grab the shopping bag, from which a pair of boots had spilled out. "I can get the phone replaced easily enough. Actually, do you know where I could do that? I'm new to town, and I don't remember seeing any electronics stores around."

She bit back a grin. "You wouldn't. We don't have any, other than a place that sells some used laptops and computers. You're going to have to drive to West Creek for that. They're about half an hour away, and they've got everything. There are a couple of phone shops there. I guess you won't be able to use your GPS to get there, but the library has free computers for everyone, whether you have a card or not, and you can print out a map for about ten cents."

"Thanks," he said. "Ah, where is the library?"

"You really are new here, aren't you?" she asked, giving him a kind smile. "You just turn right at the end of this block and walk a bit. You'll see the sign for it. They are open until five every day except for the weekends. They close Saturdays at noon, and don't open at all on Sundays."

"Thanks. I just moved here last week, and I've been settling into my new job, so I haven't really had a chance to explore. I know I said it already but thank you. Can I take you out for lunch or for coffee, or something? You saved me from a nasty accident, and you're also the first person who actually stopped and pointed me around town. I could use someone to help me get used to the area."

"It's funny that you mention coffee," she said, "because I own French Roast, which is right on Main Street. I'm there most days; I work six days a week and four of them I'm there starting at seven in the morning. The other two days, I'm there all afternoon until we close. If you get there at noon any day except for Tuesday, which is my day off, you're going to be pretty much guaranteed to find me."

"I'll stop in," he promised. "It was nice to meet you,"

"You too," she said. He bent down to scoop up the remains of his phone, then crossed the street, looking both ways this time. He paused on the other side to give her a wave. She returned it, then looked down at Latte. "You're a menace," she said. "I'm not complaining; don't get me wrong. I'm glad I saved him – but could you keep the whole following people around thing to once or twice a week? I really can't deal with the stress every day."

Latte meowed, standing up and winding around her ankles, then pawed at her legs until Lorelei bent down to scoop the cat into her arms. She began walking back down the block toward her car, glad that she had been successful in her good deed for the day.

CHAPTER ELEVEN

To her surprise, she saw Hugh again the next day. He stopped in at French Roast right at noon, like she'd suggested, and took his time ordering, gazing at the menu with something like awe. He ended up choosing a salted caramel macchiato, something she knew Alyssa would be thrilled to hear. The two of them needed to get together soon for a gossip session about the newest addition to their town. He was definitely gossip worthy, and if he was single, she got the feeling he wouldn't be for long. She shot a glance at his hand, checking to see if he was wearing a ring, and was glad to see that he wasn't. Wildborne was a small town; single newcomers always made quite a splash indeed.

He waited politely, sipping his coffee at the bar while a few other customers came and went. When she had no one else to attend to, she went over to lean against the counter across from him. He smiled and said, "Thanks for the advice yesterday. I managed to replace my phone."

"I'm glad I could help," she said. "You said you just moved to the area? What do you do?"

"I'm a wildlife photographer," he said. "The company I work for is technically located in West Creek, but since I'll be spending most of my time in the middle of nowhere taking pictures of wildlife, I figured I might as well live closer to where I'll actually be working." He winced. "I don't mean that Wildborne is the middle of nowhere. It seems like a lovely town. I don't want to offend you or anything –"

She chuckled and cut him off with a wave of her hand. "No, don't worry about it. We are kind of at the edge of civilization here. Why did you move out here for work, though?"

"Honestly? I wanted a change of pace. I've always liked the idea of living in a smaller town. I'm renting an apartment now on a month-to-month lease, but I'm looking into buying a house. I just want to give the area a try first, make sure I'm willing to commit living here for a while."

"It's similar to what I did," Lorelei said. "I opened this coffee shop a few years ago, but before that I lived in a large city. My grandmother was at the nursing home here– she passed away about six months ago – and she offered to help me set up a business. We'd always been close. I wanted to start something locally, so I ended up signing a six-month lease for an apartment while I got everything arranged. By then, I fell in love with Wildborne and knew I was going to want to stay even if the business failed. I ended up buying a house because it just made more sense financially than continuing to rent. I haven't regretted it since."

"Well, I'm glad you decided to stay," he said a smile. "If you weren't here, I probably wouldn't be either. Oh, and I wouldn't be drinking this delicious coffee right now."

She grinned and opened her mouth to respond to the compliment, but the door opened, admitting a young man who was beginning to become familiar, even though he was from out of town.

Eddie approached the counter, and she could tell by looking at his face that he was angry about something. He bit out an order for coffee and she made it in silence, just looking at him with a raised brow. When he saw her expression, he seemed to deflate a bit. "The police just took me in for questioning," he explained. "Me! Someone, I'm sure it was that nosy neighbor of hers – not you of course, the other one– told the police that she kept a spare key under the pot on her porch and I was one of the only ones who knew about it. She mentioned that she'd seen me coming and going a couple of times in the past when I was visiting, which is how she knew about it. Apparently, since there was no sign of forced entry, the police got it into their heads that I used that spare key to break into my aunt's house and kill her. I wasn't even in town at the time! I didn't get here until the morning after she died. How on earth can they suspect me?"

"I'm sure they're just trying to cover all their bases," she said, trying to soothe him as she passed the coffee over. "Take it as a good sign, that they're still looking for her killer instead of having given up. They're looking at absolutely everyone they can. It means they're taking it seriously."

"But they should be questioning people who were actually in town when she died," he said, starting to sound increasingly angry. "I probably wasn't even the only one who knew about the key; I'm sure she had other people stop in and water her plants and stuff. Or someone could have just picked the lock. She doesn't have any alarms."

"I have a key too," Lorelei said. "And actually, I do think I knew about the one under the pot – she mentioned it in passing once, but I didn't remember until just now." She remembered the smashed pot and frowned. "Did they ever find the key?"

"No," he said. "But the whole place was a mess. They let me in yesterday to see if I could catalog what was missing. It was… horrible."

She almost nodded in agreement but caught herself in time. She didn't think he would be very impressed if he knew she had been in the house as well, but not at the invitation of the police.

"They're probably onto something about the key. I doubt there are that many people who can pick locks around town."

She frowned suddenly, remembering what had been

lying on the passenger seat of Mr. Strauss's car when she stopped to make sure he was okay after he almost hit Hugh. The crystal glasses, that had nagged at her memory so much. She opened her mouth to mention it, then shut it again, glancing at Hugh. She'd only just met the guy, and she didn't want to talk about something that would make such easy fodder for rumors in front of him.

Eddie seemed to notice her inhibition, however. "What?"

"I just had an idea, but it would be best to talk about it somewhere more private."

He seemed to consider this for a second. "You really were a good friend of hers, weren't you?"

She nodded. "I know she was a lot older than me, but she was one of my best friends here in town. We talked almost every day. We had each other's backs."

"Are you interested in finding out who killed her too? Or, do you think I should just let the police do what they do, like Walker does?"

"I want to know more than anything," she admitted. "She didn't deserve what happened to her."

"If you think you might know something, why don't we meet up tonight and talk about it? You can come over to Walker's place; he has an apartment not far from here. He's going to be out tonight."

"All right," she agreed. "I'll give you my number; you can text me the address. I'll be out of here early this afternoon; I can come over any time after that."

He nodded and they exchanged numbers before he left. Hugh was watching her with curiosity but didn't ask what their conversation was about, even though he had likely heard a good amount of it, for which she was grateful. She liked him well enough so far, but even if she got to know him better, there was a lot that she wouldn't be able to tell him. Somehow, her life had gone from normal and boring enough that she didn't have any secrets to speak of, to strange enough that there were things she couldn't tell anyone, not even her own mother, and she wasn't quite sure how she felt about it.

CHAPTER TWELVE

She went home after her shift; Eddie had asked her to meet him later in the evening, when he was sure Walker would be out. It wasn't that he didn't trust his friend, he explained; it was just that Walker thought that he should leave well enough alone and let the police handle it. He didn't want to deal with his friend's complaining and figured what he didn't know wouldn't hurt him.

She took the time to shower and change into something comfortable and spend an hour or two lounging on the couch with Latte, who seemed a bit irritated with her for leaving her home that day.

"Life has been kind of crazy lately," she said as she

stroked the cat's soft fur. "I just couldn't deal with chasing after you again today. I'm sorry. I'll bring you with me tomorrow."

At last, Latte began to purr and Lorelei felt better; she hated feeling as if her cat was mad at her.

At last, six o'clock rolled around and she got up, opening a can of food for Latte and scooping it into her dish before leaving, making sure the door was shut and firmly locked behind her. She shot a glance at Mrs. Whittaker's house as she went, as had become habit for her. Seeing the empty home with the crime scene tape strung across the door made her heart ache, and she walked forward with more certainty. Maybe between her and Eddie, they could figure out why his aunt had been killed.

She parked along the road in town and made her way up to the top of the shop apartment that Eddie had given her the address for. She knocked and waited only a few seconds before he opened the door, letting her in. He shut it behind her, then led her to the living room. The decor was low cost, but it was relatively tidy, and she perched on the couch happily enough. She set her purse down without looking, and it tumbled off the table. The spare GPS tracker fell out of it and she picked it up with a sigh; she had almost forgotten about it, and really should put it somewhere safer. She slipped it into her pocket, knowing she would feel it there when she got home.

"You had an idea at the coffee shop, I could tell. What was it?" he asked, jumping right to the point.

"It's just… you know those pretty crystal glasses your aunt had? The ones that sat in the display case in her dining room?"

"The ones she never ever used?" He snorted. "Yeah. I remember when I was a kid, I used to think they were made out of diamonds. I thought crystal and diamond were the same thing, for some reason. I thought she would be rich if she sold them. My dad told me how much my mom's engagement ring cost once, and I figured if a diamond that small was so expensive, a diamond as big as those glasses were would be worth a fortune."

"Well, they probably were worth a pretty penny. The crystal glasses are one of the things someone stole."

"How do you know that?" he asked, narrowing his eyes at her.

She winced and backed up. "You know how I said I had a spare key? I… may have gone into her house, just to see what happened, and to see if maybe there would be anything there that would help me figure it all out. I didn't touch anything, and I don't think I did anything that would affect the investigation."

"All right," he said slowly, not looking quite convinced but willing to hear her out.

"Anyway, I noticed a lot of her stuff was missing; her jewelry, which I helped her sort and untangle a while ago, the nice silverware, which she used when she invited me over for lunch the weekend after my grandmother died, and those crystal glasses. One looked like it had fallen and broken, but the rest were gone. Anyway, yesterday, I managed to stop Hugh – the guy who was sitting at the counter while we were talking at the coffee shop – from getting run over by the locksmith's truck. His name is Gerald Strauss; have you met him?"

He shook his head.

"Well, he had to come to your aunt's house a few times, until he finally just suggested that she make a couple of spare keys. She did that; she gave me one and she hid one under the plant pot, as you know. But he knew how to get into her house; he knew it very well. And no one would think twice of his truck; he's the only locksmith in town and people call him whenever they lock themselves out of the house or car. And I wouldn't have thought anything of it either, except for yesterday, after he almost hit Hugh, Mr. Strauss stopped and asked if he was okay. I went over to the window to talk to him and I noticed on the passenger seat he had a box with bubble wrap in it, and what looked like a set of crystal glasses identical to your aunt's. I was distracted from the near accident, so I didn't make the connection right away, but now I'm almost sure of it."

Eddie fell silent, realization slowly coming to his eyes. "You think he's the one who did it? Why would he?"

"Well, I don't know. I guess it's possible he was having money problems or something. I know she invited him in for tea after he unlocked the door for her as thanks at least once. If he knew how to get in without breaking the windows or forcing his way through the door, he might've thought he could steal stuff without her even noticing while she was sleeping. Like I said, I don't really have much knowledge of what happened other than the memory of the glasses on his passenger seat. They might not even have been the same ones, but something you mentioned about how either the person who broke in had a key or could pick locks stuck with me."

"Are you going to tell the police about it?" he asked. "I think you should, for what it's worth. They can question him, at least, and maybe search his house; they could see if he has the stuff she's missing there."

"I don't know. Like I said, it's all just conjecture. I don't want to get him in trouble if he's innocent."

"But what if he's not innocent?" Eddie asked, leaning forward. "If he's the one who killed my aunt… He's got to face some sort of punishment for it. She was one of the kindest people I knew."

"Me too," Lorelei said, sighing. "I just don't know what to do. I don't want to make things worse for anyone. For all I know, he bought the glasses in a pawnshop."

Eddie blinked slowly, frowning. "Do you think the killer would have sold her things already? Wouldn't that be risky?"

She raised her hands in an expression of defeat. "Don't ask me. I'm scrambling to try to make sense of all this, just like you are. I don't know anything about selling stuff to pawn shops or how sales are tracked."

"I guess whoever killed her must have planned the break-in prior to it. They could already have had somewhere set up to sell the items, maybe even out of town. If they knew her well, they would have had a good idea of exactly what they would come away with. It all keeps coming back to someone who knew her."

"I just realized I'm probably at the top of your suspect list," Lorelei said, wincing. "I knew her well, I was at her house a lot, and I had a spare key."

Eddie seemed to consider her for a moment. "I mean, I guess you check all of the boxes, but I don't really think you did it. No offense, but you don't exactly seem like the murderous type."

"I promise you I'm not," Lorelei said. "Though Marigold did accuse me of it, so I guess not everyone sees me that way."

"Marigold?" he asked.

"She's Mrs. Whittaker's other neighbor."

"Oh," he said, a look of realization coming into his eyes. "Her. I didn't know her name. She's... not exactly the most pleasant woman."

"No, she's not," Lorelei said. "And she was there the night of the murder. In fact, she was the one who found her."

His eyes widened. "Why didn't anyone tell me this? Do you think she's the one who did it? I wouldn't put it past her from what I remember of her, the few times she's spoken of me."

"It could be her," Lorelei admitted slowly. "But... I don't think it is. I could maybe see her stabbing someone in a fit of anger, but I really can't see her sinking so low as to steal something for money. I agree that she's not the most pleasant person, but she does have her own sort of pride."

"Still… I don't want to take her off of this list we're making just yet. So far, we have the locksmith and your neighbor. I think we can agree that neither of us are secretly thinking the other is the killer?"

"Well, like you said, you weren't even in town, and she was my friend."

He nodded. "Do you know of anyone else?"

"Not really," Lorelei said. "I think Marigold's the only person in the world who didn't like Mrs. Whittaker, so I doubt she had any enemies. I also can't think of anyone else who would've been able to get into the house so easily. Do you know if there's anyone you told about the spare key?"

"No, just—" He paused, his eyes widening slightly. "She went on a trip after Christmas to visit her sister, who lives in a retirement community in Florida, and she asked me to swing by to check everything out. She offered to let me stay the weekend in the empty house and get a mini vacation myself, since it's a bit of a drive for me. I think you were away for the weekend or something, and she wanted to make sure her plants got watered. Anyway, I took a friend with me. He saw me take the key out from under the pot, and he walked around the house with me. I even sent him off on his own to water some plants."

"Who was the friend?"

He swallowed. "Walker."

CHAPTER THIRTEEN

"I would never suspect him. It's just... he's not working right now, but he's had a weird amount of cash lately. He keeps paying for stuff... for example, he got the pizza the other night even though I offered to buy it, and you saw him get the coffee the other day. I mean, I'm the one crashing with him while I deal with my aunt's funeral. I should be buying the pizzas and drinks as a thank you. It's almost like he feels... guilty or something."

"And the other day, he pretty much told you to give up on the police ever catching the person who killed her," Lorelei mused. "I didn't say anything then, since it wasn't really my business, but it was almost like he didn't want the killer to get caught."

Eddie frowned, his expression going from angry to worried and hurt in just moments. "I can't... I can't really be thinking of accusing my friend, can I? I mean, we went to school together. We've kept in touch even after I moved away. He wouldn't... He wouldn't do something like that."

"I don't think you would have brought him up if part of you didn't think he might," she said gently.

He hesitated but nodded. "You're right. What do we do now?"

"We need proof," she said. "You can't accuse anyone without proof, especially not your friend."

"He shouldn't be back for little while yet. I think... I think I'm going to look through his room. You don't need to stay and help, but..."

"I'll stay," she said. She still felt like this was all her fault, in a way. If only she had taken Latte's warning seriously... She shook her head. She couldn't think about that now.

He nodded, his face pale, and stood up, walking down the hall and reaching for the right-hand door. There didn't appear to be a lock on the door, and it opened easily. The room inside was a bit messier than the rest of the apartment was, but still nothing terrible. He looked around, and Lorelei shifted awkwardly. It was one thing to talk about searching someone's things for proof that he had murdered an old lady, but actually doing it made her feel uncomfortable. She wouldn't want anyone digging through her stuff, after all.

"I guess I'll start... I'll get the bedside table and desk. Do you want the closet?"

"All right," she said. Not happy with the situation, but feeling as if she could hardly stop now, she walked over to the closet and opened it. There were a few clothes hanging up and a jumbled pile on the floor. Hoping Walker was just as slow to put away clean laundry as she was and didn't leave all of his dirty clothes in a pile in his closet, she began poking through his things. She could hear Eddie rustling through the desk behind her.

She was about to give it up and call it a loss when, at the bottom of the pile of clothes in the closet, she unearthed a box. It was a simple shoebox, but the weight told her that there was something inside it. She opened it slowly and let out a gasp when she saw the pile of jewelry inside. She didn't know Mrs. Whittaker's belongings well enough to recognize every piece, but she certainly recognized a few. On top of the jewelry, were a few receipts. She saw they were from a pawn shop in a city about an hour away, recording the sale of the crystal glasses and the silverware.

"Eddie," she said. "Eddie, come look at this."

"Look at what?" a voice from the door asked. She jumped, and the shoebox fell from her hands, the jewelry spilling everywhere. Walker was standing at the bedroom door, staring at them both with an inscrutable expression on his face. She hadn't heard him come into the apartment and realized, too late, that one of them should have kept watch.

Eddie straightened up from the other side of the bed, where he must have been digging through the nightstand. He glanced at his friend, then slid his eyes over to her. She could spot when he saw the jewelry, because his face paled even further before his gaze snapped back to Walker. "I didn't know you were home, man," he said.

"Obviously. I didn't know you were planning on snooping through my room while I was gone."

"We didn't plan on it, we just –"

"I let you stay with me because we were friends. This is how you're going to repay me? Going through my stuff?"

"Walker, there's a box full of jewelry in your closet. Can you explain it?"

There was a plaintive note in his voice that, to Lorelei, sounded like he really wanted the other man to explain it all away. She straightened up slowly, not sure what she should do.

"I don't know where it came from," Walker said, shrugging. "It was probably my mom's or something; I must've just forgotten about it."

"I recognize this ruby necklace," Lorelei said. "Mrs. Whittaker's husband gave it to her for their fiftieth anniversary. She loved it." She picked up the piece she had mentioned and held it up to the light. Walker flinched.

"Look, it's not what you think –"

"Not what I think?" Eddie asked, stepping forward. "You killed my aunt, Walker. There's not really anything you can say that would make it better."

"I never meant to kill her," Walker said. "I meant to just get in and out. You told me how heavily she sleeps, that she takes medication and that you worried about her not waking up if there was an emergency. But she was in the kitchen when I unlocked the door – she didn't even turn on the lights, she was just getting something out of the fridge. She saw me and I just — I just panicked. I knew she'd recognize me, and I didn't want to get in trouble. I regretted it right away, but it wasn't like I could say anything to anyone. She was already dead by the time I realized what I'd done and confessing to it wouldn't do anything except get me in prison."

"I can't believe you even broke in in the first place. Even if killing her was an accident, you planned to rob a little old lady, Walker. I can't believe we were ever even friends. Get out of my way."

"Where are you going?" Walker said, moving to block him.

"I'm going to call the police and tell them exactly what happened."

"No, you're not," Walker said. He put his hands out and shoved Eddie back. Lorelei hurried forward without thinking, hoping to be able to keep the two men from fighting. Instead of moving toward Eddie though, Walker turned and grabbed her, looping an arm around her neck. "Neither of you are going to do anything. I don't want to hurt you, Eddie, man, but I'm not taking the fall for this."

He began backing away, dragging Lorelei after him. Frantically, wondering if he already had a plan in place to escape or if he was just going to drive and not stop until he ran out of cash, she reached into her pocket where she had put the second GPS tracker after it fell out of her purse, and purposefully stumbled. He had to readjust his grip to catch her, and she took advantage of the moment to slip the tracker into his pocket. For a moment, she thought he had noticed, as his grip tightened on her, but she realized instead that they had reached the front door and he was pausing to unlock it. He hesitated, then said, "Give me your phones."

When Eddie hesitated, he tightened his grip on her. "Give them to me, now."

Eddie dug his cell phone out of his pocket and then looked at Lorelei questioningly. "It's in my purse," she gasped, trying to pull Walker's arm away from her throat.

He dug through it and finally pulled it out, handing both over to Walker, who took them in his free hand. He dropped them immediately and stomped on both until the screens cracked.

"You're going to give me at least half an hour to get away, all right? Neither of you will ever see me again. I'm sorry, Eddie, I really am. If I could go back in time, I wouldn't do it again, but I'm not going to spend the rest of my life in prison for one mistake."

With that, he shoved Lorelei hard enough that she stumbled and crashed to the floor. When she looked up, Walker was gone. Eddie looked at the broken phones, then back to where his friend had vanished.

"We should go to the neighbors," he said. "I don't know what his plan is, but I don't want him getting away."

"You don't have to worry about that," Lorelei said. "As soon as we get to a computer, we can track him." At his questioning look, she explained about the GPS tracker, and he seemed recovered enough to give her a faint smile.

"Well, I'm sorry I got you involved in all of this, but I've got to admit, I'm glad I did. Thank you, Lorelei. Figuring out Walker killed her won't bring my aunt back, but it will help her to rest in peace."

EPILOGUE

Lorelei drizzled the caramel sauce and sprinkled a pinch of sea salt over the top of the whipped cream, then slid the mug carefully across the counter to her friend. "There you go, Alyssa. This is only your eighth one this week. I'm proud."

"You are amazing, Lorelei," Alyssa said, taking a sip of it. "Despite how grateful I am, though, you shouldn't be here."

Lorelei shrugged. It had only been a couple of days since the fiasco with Eddie and Walker, and she hadn't even taken the next morning off. She was exhausted, but not in the sort of way an extra few hours' sleep would help. "Tomorrow is my day off," she said. "I'll relax then."

"How are you such a workaholic?"

"I'm not," Lorelei said. "You should see my to-do list. It keeps getting bigger and bigger. I just like being here because I know it's something I can do well. It's like, with all the chaos in my life recently, this is what calms me down. I come in here, I make coffee for people, I pop a batch of croissants or muffins or whatever into the oven, and it makes the world a better place. There is nothing dangerous or stressful or even that exciting about it. Plus, if I was sitting at home, I would just feel guilty about making someone take over my shift at the last minute."

"You're crazy, but you seem happy, I'll give you that," her friend said. "I still wish you'd tell me more about why you felt like you had to get involved with all the stuff with Mrs. Whittaker."

"I know, and I'm sorry, but I can't explain it. I just felt like it was all my fault, somehow. I wanted to do something to help make it right."

"Well, you caught a murderer. That definitely counts for something."

"Yeah, I guess it does." Lorelei gave her friend a smile, then her gaze drifted over to Latte, who was happily curled up in her bed. She still had the GPS tracker on her collar, but Lorelei hadn't had to use it yet. She knew the next time her cat vanished, she would be back out there, trying to figure out who needed saving and from what. But for now, she was happy just to sip coffee, talk to her friend, and enjoy the feeling that her life was finally settling into its new normal.

AUTHOR'S NOTE

I'd love to hear your thoughts on my books, the storylines, and anything else that you'd like to comment on—reader feedback is very important to me. My contact information, along with some other helpful links, is listed on the next page. If you'd like to be on my list of "folks to contact" with updates, release and sales notifications, etc.… just shoot me an email and let me know. Thanks for reading!

Also…

… if you're looking for more great reads, Summer Prescott Books publishes several popular series by outstanding Cozy Mystery authors.

CONTACT SUMMER PRESCOTT BOOKS PUBLISHING

Twitter: @summerprescott1

Bookbub: https://www.bookbub.com/authors/summer-prescott

Blog and Book Catalog: http://summerprescottbooks.com

Email: summer.prescott.cozies@gmail.com

YouTube: https://www.youtube.com/channel/UCngKNUkDdWuQ5k7-Vkfrp6A

And…be sure to check out the Summer Prescott Cozy Mysteries fan page and Summer Prescott Books Publishing Page on Facebook – let's be friends!

CONTACT SUMMER PRESCOTT BOOKS PUBLISHING

To download a free book, and sign up for our fun and exciting newsletter, which will give you opportunities to win prizes and swag, enter contests, and be the first to know about New Releases, click here: http://summerprescottbooks.com